School Day Adventure

For my sister, Debbie —P. H.

To Eric —K. M.

SIMON SPOTLIGHT
An imprint of Simon & Schuster Children's Publishing Division
1230 Avenue of the Americas
New York, New York 10020
This Simon Spotlight edition October 2015
Text and illustrations copyright © 2000 by Simon & Schuster, Inc.
The names and depictions of Raggedy Ann and Raggedy Andy are trademarks of Simon & Schuster, Inc.
All rights reserved, including the right of reproduction in whole or in part in any form.
SIMON SPOTLIGHT, READY-TO-READ, and colophon are registered trademarks of Simon & Schuster, Inc.
For information about special discounts for bulk purchases, please contact Simon & Schuster Special Sales at
1-866-506-1949 or business@simonandschuster.com
Manufactured in the United States of America 0915 LAK
2 4 6 8 10 9 7 5 3 1
Library of Congress Cataloging-in-Publication Data
Hall, Patricia, 1948-
School day adventure / by Patricia Hall ; illustrated by Kathryn Mitter.
p. cm. — (Classic Raggedy Ann & Andy) (Ready-to-read)
Summary: When Marcella takes Raggedy Ann and Andy to school for show-and-tell, they meet some other
interesting characters, including Mac the truck and Petunia the guinea pig.
[1. Schools—Fiction. 2. Dolls—Fiction. 3. Toys—Fiction. 4. Show-and-tell presentations—Fiction.]
I. Mitter, Kathy, ill. II. Title. III. Series. IV. Series: Ready-to-read
PZ7.H147515 Sf 2000
[E]—dc21 99-056168
ISBN 978-1-4814-5089-8 (hc)
ISBN 978-1-4814-5088-1 (pbk)
ISBN 978-1-4814-5090-4 (eBook)
RaggedyAnnBooks.com

F ... IN & ANDY
School Day Adventure

by Patricia Hall
illustrated by Kathryn Mitter

Ready-to-Read

Simon Spotlight
New York   London   Toronto   Sydney   New Delhi

It was show-and-tell day at school. All the children had special things to share. Marcella had brought her Raggedy Ann and Andy dolls.

Debbie shared first. "This is Petunia, my real live guinea pig," said Debbie. "She eats lettuce and chews on hay. And sometimes at night she goes 'squeak squeak.'"

"This is my new truck," said Marty. "His name is Mac. He says 'vroom vroom,' and he can go and can carry things. But only if I help."

Then it was Marcella's turn.

"These are my rag dolls, Raggedy Ann and Raggedy Andy," she said. "They aren't alive. And they can't eat or carry things.

But Raggedy Andy can put his feet all the
way over his shoulders. And Raggedy Ann
has a real candy heart that says 'I Love You.'"

"Wonderful show-and-tell, boys and girls!" said Ms. Kelly. "Now, put away your things, and let's put on our alphabet thinking caps. Yesterday we learned about the letter 'J.' Who knows what comes next?"

"K!" said Josie.

"Right!" said Ms. Kelly. "And what begins with K?"

"Kitten!" said Pablo.

"Kite!" said David.

"Kelly!" said Marcella. "Ms. Kelly!"

"Right again!" said Ms. Kelly. "Your thinking caps are really working! Now let's get ready for lunch."

After the children had gone to the cafeteria, the classroom became very, very quiet.

But then there was a rustle inside Marcella's cubby.

"Hey," said Raggedy Ann, stretching her rag-doll arms.

"Hey, yourself," said Raggedy Andy,
uncurling his rag-doll legs.

"Hay's for horses—and sometimes me!"
said a squeaky voice from across the room.
It was Debbie's guinea pig, Petunia.

"I didn't know guinea pigs could talk!" said
Raggedy Ann.

"Of course we can," squeaked Petunia.
"But I didn't know rag dolls could walk!"

"You bet we can!" answered Raggedy Andy.
"But only when human beans aren't around."

"He means human beings," explained
Raggedy Ann.

"Do you really like lettuce and hay like Debbie said?" Raggedy Ann asked.

"As long as I get lots of water to drink," answered Petunia. "Hay makes me thirsty."

"Oh!" laughed Raggedy Ann. "I could never drink water. My candy heart would melt completely away!"

Just then the Raggedys heard a gulp and a splash. "Hello-o-o!" came a bubbly voice. "I'm Gill."

"Hi there!" said the soft voice of the teddy bear. "My name is Teddy, and this is Leo. We love having visitors in Ms. Kelly's classroom."

"Nice to meet you!" said the Raggedys and Petunia at the same time.

"What is a classroom, anyway?" asked
Raggedy Andy. "Is it like Marcella's
playroom?"

"Not exactly," said Raggedy Ann gently.

"A classroom is where we are now—where everyone wears a thinking cap."

Raggedy Andy reached up. Was this his thinking cap?

Just then there was a *vroom vroom* and a *honk honk*. Out of Marty's cubby rolled Mac the truck.

"Greetings!" he said.

"Wow!" said Raggedy Andy. "I thought you couldn't go unless Marty helped you."

"Oh, yeah?" said Mac. "Hop in!"

"Leaving so soon?" gulped Gill.

"Watch out for the table leg!" warned Teddy.

"Have a great time!" squeaked Petunia.

"Hang on!" cried Mac. "We're rolling now!"

"This is fun!" laughed Raggedy Ann. She loved to ride in the car.

"Phew!" said Raggedy Andy. "That was a close one!"

"Mac! Watch out!" cried out Raggedy Andy.

Raggedy Ann stepped on the brakes. Mac rolled to a stop.

"Wow!" said Mac. "Close call! Maybe we should be getting back."

"You're right," said Raggedy Ann after a moment. "But how? All the doors look alike."

"Gosh," said Raggedy Andy. "Look at all of them. I wish I knew how to read."

Then Raggedy Andy remembered his thinking cap! As soon as he put it on, he felt smarter. "Look!" he cried. "The letter 'K'!"

"The one for kitten and kite?" asked Raggedy Ann.

"Yes!" said Raggedy Andy. "And Kelly!
Ms. Kelly starts with the letter 'K'!"

Now Mac and the Raggedys knew just
where to go.

"They're back!" squeaked Petunia.

"Finally," gulped Gill.

"Are we glad to see you!" said Teddy and Leo together.

"Quick!" said Mac. "I hear the children!"

The class came in that very minute.

"We just made it!" whispered Raggedy Ann.

Later that night at home, Marcella gave the
Raggedys an extra-special good-night hug. "I
was proud of you at show-and-tell today," she
said.

The Raggedys didn't say a word. They waited quietly until all the lights were out and Marcella had gone to bed.

Then Raggedy Ann and Andy told the other
dolls all about their exciting day at school.

"Weren't you scared?" asked the Camel
with the Wrinkled Knees, when he heard
about the Raggedys' ride with Mac.

"Oh, no," said Raggedy Andy. "We had a lot of fun!"

"I'll bet it was fun!" said Uncle Clem. He loved adventure.

"It was until we got lost," said Raggedy Ann.

"How did you find your way back?"
asked the Camel with the Wrinkled Knees.

"Easy," grinned Raggedy Andy. "I just put
on my thinking cap!"

And with that, the dolls said good night and
fell asleep with their shoe-button eyes wide
open, the way rag dolls always do.